Among the Blacks

ALSO BY RAYMOND ROUSSEL :

La Doublure (1897)
Impressions d'Afrique (1910)
Locus Solus (1914)
La Poussière de Soleils (1927)
Nouvelles Impressions d'Afrique (1932)
Comment j'ai écrit certains de mes livres (1935)

Selected works in translation :
Impressions of Africa, translated by Rayner Heppenstall
 and Lindy Ford (University of California, 1967)
Locus Solus, translated by Rupert Copeland Cunningham
 (University of California, 1970)
How I Wrote Certain of My Books, translated by Trevor
 Winkfield (SUN, 1977)

ALSO BY RON PADGETT :

Bean Spasms, with Ted Berrigan (Kulchur, 1967)
Great Balls of Fire (Holt, Rinehart and Winston, 1969)
Toujours l'amour (SUN, 1976)
Tulsa Kid (Z Press, 1979)
Triangles in the Afternoon (SUN, 1979)
How to Be a Woodpecker (Toothpaste, 1983)

Selected translations :
Pierre Cabanne, *Dialogues with Marcel Duchamp* (Viking, 1971)
Blaise Cendrars, *Kodak* (Adventures in Poetry, 1976)
Valery Larbaud, *The Poems of A. O. Barnabooth,*
 with Bill Zavatsky (Mushinsha Ltd., 1977)
Guillaume Apollinaire, *The Poet Assassinated and Other Stories*
 (North Point, 1984)

Among the Blacks

Two Works

Raymond Roussel
_____
Ron Padgett

Avenue B

Cover by Trevor Winkfield

Raymond Roussel's "Parmi les noirs" was published in his book
Comment j'ai écrit certains de mes livres (Lemerre, 1935; new edition,
as part of his his *Oeuvres Complètes,* Jean-Jacques Pauvert, 1962).
Earlier versions of Ron Padgett's translation of "Among the Blacks"
appeared in *Bones* and *Juillard.*

Distributed by:
SMALL PRESS DISTRIBUTION, 1814 San Pablo Ave., Berkeley, CA 94702
SUN & MOON PRESS, P.O. Box 481170, Los Angeles, CA 90048
THE SEGUE FOUNDATION, 300 Bowery, New York, NY 10012

Avenue B
P.O. Box 542
Bolinas, CA 94924

To Lorenzo Thomas and Dick Gallup

Contents

Among the Blacks

RAYMOND ROUSSEL

THE WHITE LETTERS on the bands of the old pooltable formed an incomprehensible combination. I was already on my sixth trip around it, delighted by the words I had obtained with my system, which was nevertheless so simple.

"What gibberish!" I thought. No one would find the key. Even Balancier would be completely baffled by it.

He's an interesting sort, this Balancier. In his youth he had already written some verse pieces of great promise and quality. I had been very much taken with the simplicity and stylistic vigor of his first novel. I had sent him word of my good impression, and the response I received the very next day overflowed with gratitude and congeniality. Then two years with no news of Balancier. But one morning I received a parcel from a publisher, a new book by him, entitled *Among the Blacks.* At the top of the first page a few dedicatory words doubled, for me, the book's value.

Among the Blacks is about a master mariner named White, who embarks one day from Brest. His wife and

five-year-old son weep as they say goodbye, staying on
board until the last moment. Finally the time comes. The
wife and child return to the dock and the boat sails off into
the distance.

Good weather favors the crossing during the first
week. But on the eighth day a terrible storm is unleashed.
The boat, torn to pieces, is about to founder at any moment. The entire crew take their places in the longboats.
Despite their entreaties, White alone refuses to abandon
ship. He watches his companions go off rapidly into the
distance, and soon he loses sight of them. A gust of wind
breaks the mast, which falls and strikes him on the head.
He sinks unconscious to the deck. When he returns to his
senses, he finds himself surrounded by Negroes, who are
dressing his wounds. His boat, stranded on a beach, is just
a heap of wreckage barely held together. Nevertheless,
part of the cargo is still good, and other Negroes, more
numerous, are carrying away objects of all sorts on their
backs.

After several days, White recovers. He goes to find
the black chief, a terrible old man they call the "Booltable." By means of a clever pantomime, White makes it
understood that he should very much like to leave. The
Booltable becomes angry and orders that White be kept

under surveillance. And so begins a nomadic life of hard-
ship and danger. With an iron hand, the Booltable rules
veritable black hordes, sacking everything he finds in his
way. White becomes certain, studying the flora and fauna,
that he is crossing Central Africa. He is the object of
continuous surveillance, because the Booltable depends on
him for his intelligence and education, which he does not
fail to use every day.

Without ever getting used to it, White witnesses end-
less new cruelties. As soon as a village is sighted, the
Booltable attacks it with his innumerable troops, who
quickly overcome it. Then follow hideous scenes of canni-
balism. The old are spared no more than the infants and
adults, and the Booltable is the first to make a feast of this
human flesh. All those who are spared are taken as re-
cruits. All possible plunder is seized, and fire is set to the
four corners of the unfortunate hamlet. What does White
do during the hours of respite this trying life sometimes
leaves him? He draws from the provision of paper, pens,
and ink the Negroes found while stripping his ship; and
he writes. . . . He writes to his wife, whom he will perhaps
never see again, the wife who doubtless thinks him already dead. He wants her always to have hope and never
to forget him. The pages are quickly filled with details of

the deeds and exploits of the Booltable and his savage
armies. The project is accelerated only when the poor cap-
tive decides to finish it. He places it all in a strong envelope
and writes his wife's address on it in thick letters. Then he
goes over to a large cage filled with all sorts of birds, which
he has caught in a trap. He chooses from them the strong-
est and most beautiful. After caressing it for a moment, as
if to teach it caution, he attaches the envelope to its neck
and sets it free. And it is with a heavy beating of his heart
that he watches it fly away and disappear.

Almost every day White uses this method to tell his
wife of his terrible adventures. It is a sort of diary.

Now, these lively and imaginative accounts form the
sole matter of *Among the Blacks*. In the first account,
White spoke of the moment of separation, the crossing,
and then of the shipwreck and his "return to life" among
the blacks. The second account was devoted to a portrait
of the Booltable, "a great old man black as ebony, with
a fierce and bloodthirsty face, who with a single gesture
terrifies the thousands of savages he drags behind him."
Next came the first atrocities White witnessed. And,
throughout the volume, one was able to follow him across
the unexplored regions where the Booltable was able to
satisfy his ferocious instincts. Dating each account helped

structure the whole work. As a conclusion, Balancier made his hero escape and undergo new dangers, finally to be welcomed by some European travelers returning to the civilized countries of the coast. White himself recounts this happy denouement in his last epistle. Before signing it, he wrote "See you soon" to his wife and son, because his return could no longer be doubted, now that he was among his own kind.

I had not seen Balancier since more than a month after I had finished *Among the Blacks*. And so I was delighted to find him with my good friend and colleague Flambeau, who had invited me to spend a week with him at his country house. I was able to thank Balancier again for his parcel and to discuss with him the most minute details of his work.

Now, it was pouring rain that day, and Flambeau, the attentive master of his house, had looked for an agreeable method of passing the afternoon without our going outdoors.

There were about ten of us in the drawing room. Flambeau proposed a game that promised to keep us busy for a good while. It consisted of this. A question in writing was posed to someone, then this person was shut up in an adjoining room; after exactly ten minutes the door was

opened again, and the person had to give his response in
the form of a riddle. The first to guess the riddle was
placed on "the stand" in his turn, and it was to him that
the next question was posed.

To begin, lots were drawn. All our names were placed
in a hat. Flambeau took charge of drawing one out. He
pulled out a card and read: "Débarras."

Dressed in his eternal maroon velvet suit, the poor
painter looked shabbier than ever. He was asked in writing
if he preferred watercolor or pastel, and the reasons for
his preference. In the room adjoining the drawing room,
Gauffre and Balancier were in the process of discussing a
difficult carom; Gauffre held that one must attack with
the red ball; Balancier held to the white. We asked the two
players to return to the drawing room so we could isolate
Débarras in the billard room. Flambeau checked the time.
At the end of the tenth minute, he went to the door and
Débarras brought us the riddle, which was immediately
handed around. For my part, I didn't understand very
much of it. It began with a drawing of a half of a mouth,
after which trailed a minus sign with a precise *L*. Then
came a stave with the note *re* indicated. This was followed
by the words "Not dark!" Particularly vexing was the
drawing of a man shouting "Eureka!" as he beheld a spin-

ning object that resembled a stomach, with lines emerging from its spout. Then followed a Gothic script that read "Ben ――― and gone." Then a drawing of a band around a man's neck; an insect with a large stinger on its bottom; several automobiles; a man's face in the act of shouting; a stick figure with contorted limbs, over which rose a little cloud enclosing the word "foaming"; a rectangle with "The End" in its center; a large, thick *S*; a hand; the same stinging insect, a plus sign, and a right hand. The entire series was concluded by a stout arrow running back up the page and indicating the band about the neck. It didn't take me long to give up. I handed the paper to Madame Hunch, who was sitting next to me. She took barely two minutes to reach the solution, and in a straightforward manner she read aloud: "I prefer watercolor because of its finesse and bright color."

Débarras nodded and Madame Hunch began again, having us follow on the drawing: "IP RE FAIR WATT HUR COLLAR BEE CARS O FITS FIN S hAND BEE-RIGHT COLLAR."

Because Madame Hunch had solved it, it was her turn to be questioned. Flambeau gave her a new piece of paper on which he had just written these words: "Describe a picture you would like to paint."

After eight minutes in isolation, Madame Hunch returned on her own with a second riddle.

When it was passed to me, certain things leaped immediately to my eye. First, there was a man's face, split in
half, the right side of which was utterly fiendish and ugly.
This was followed by an eyeball, from which hung an L.
Then came a skeleton key that was inserting itself into a 2.
After this there was a stack of currency in bills; the Greek
letter for alpha; the words "The Chrononhotonthologos
Man"; a cat; the incomplete group of words "– – – – –
– – – your rocker!"; a table setting that included a promi-
nent frankfurter and a jar; and last, four zebras singing in
unison, "We don't want to 'zzzz!' "

After a moment of reflection, I had the complete
sentence and I related it in detail while having the others
follow on the drawing: "HYDE L EYE KE TWO DOUgh A
CAREY CAT YOU'RE OFF MUSTARD ZEBRAS."

And I repeated fluently : "I'd like to do a caricature of
Mister Débarras."

Everyone started laughing, Débarras the very first.
His bizarre expression certainly justified Madame Hunch's
wish. But I had forgotten that it was my turn. Flambeau
had to remind me while handing me the question he had
just formulated.

When I was alone, I looked at my watch and started
thinking. Here is what Flambeau had written on the paper :

"What is, according to you, the most impressive book published this year?"

Immediately I thought of *Among the Blacks*.

"But I don't know how to draw," I said to myself. How could I follow two professionals like Débarras and Madame Hunch?

It was then that the idea of a cryptogram came to me. The three billiard balls were still in their places for the carom shot that Gauffre and Balancier had been discussing when we interrupted them. I picked up one of the small cubes of chalk lying there. I had seen Balancier carefully using it before his shot, during which time he spoke in favor of the white.

Then I began writing handsome capital letters on the green cloth, which was worn and discolored in spots. But, instead of arranging my sentence in the normal order, I wrote a capital letter on the first side, then another on the second, and another on the third and fourth; after which I returned to the first, and so on, which gave a completely unintelligible result. After six times around I had four words, each as preposterous as the other, and the more I went the more jumbled it became.

Finally, after having counted ten and three-quarters turns, I stopped and felt a bit giddy. Taking out my watch,

I saw that I was a half minute early; I opened the door and
saw Flambeau on his way toward me. I invited everyone
in and pointed to where I had placed my answer.

There was plenty of room for everyone to search at
the same time. On the first side was:

THLENBSHDLL

On the second:

HIERTAOEBTE

On the third:

ETTSHNFOOA

And on the fourth:

WETOEDTLOB

After walking around the table for a moment, Balancier seemed to have an idea. He took a notebook and
pencil out of his pocket and began to copy the four enig-
matic words. Then, leaving the others to wrack their brains,
he withdrew to a corner to concentrate. Soon his face
brightened and I saw his lips carefully articulate several
words.

"He has the key," I said to myself, "it's just a matter
of seconds now."

In fact, at that moment Balancier shot me a knowing
glance and announced that he had solved the riddle.

He showed the four words he had written, one right

below the other, while explaining that consequently it sufficed to read from top to bottom to have the true order of the sentence.

Then, addressing himself to Flambeau, he said, "Would you like to refresh our minds with the exact wording of the question?"

Flambeau repeated from memory, "What is, according to you, the most impressive book published this year?"

Everyone had read *Among the Blacks.* Hence my response was easily understood when Balancier, pencil in hand, slowly spelled out in his notebook:

"THE... WHITE... LETTERS... ON... THE... BANDS... OF... THE... OLD... BOOLTABLE."

—Translated from the French by Ron Padgett

Among the Blacks

RON PADGETT

Kaka poule pa bé.
—Creole proverb

I JUST CLEARED MY THROAT, as if I were about to say something aloud.

•

My first memory of a black person is of what was then called a "niggerman," his rain-streaked face in the night lit by a flash of lightning as my mother glances toward the bedroom window and screams. When she ran to tell my father, I had an intense flash of the scene, but in my vision the niggerman's eyes were round and white and his mouth wide open as he too screams in terror.

The first black person I knew was Berry. Whether or not that was his first name or his last he knew not. He was just Berry. He also didn't know how old he was. There were no records and his relatives didn't know. He was a large man who wore blue overalls, a longsleeve shirt, work shoes, and a straw cowboy hat. A red bandana trailed out of his hip pocket. He was very dark brown, with blue-gray eyes that reminded me of the ball bearings in the wheels of the lawn mower he pushed, and he had a quiet, powerful bass voice that came from deep inside him in quick, halting bursts.

In the growing season he walked to and from our house, over three miles each way. He tended the lawns and gardens of five or six families, taking care of a different one each day of the week. My parents had hired him because they thought that one of the first things you do after you rise above poverty level is to hire a gardener. And so, around the end of World War II, when I was three or four, this enormous black man appeared. He probably scared me with his color and size and quietness. I grew up in a family that had felt its racial prejudice harden during the Tulsa race riots of 1921. The riots had also set black Tulsans back thirty years by driving out their most dynamic community builders. It seemed that the only ones left behind were the illiterate (like Berry, who could neither read nor write even his own name); the marginally employed, those creatures who lived over in Niggertown in "chicken shacks," drove purple Buicks and Cadillacs, and drank whiskey; and the respectable poor, the church-going Christians. My parents looked down on black people, but they treated Berry with courtesy.

At the age of six I learned that he was easygoing and good-natured. One day, as he was mowing our front lawn,

I jumped out from behind a tree and shouted, "Berry! Berry! You're a *black*berry!" It was my first pun. When I told my mother, she scolded me for rudeness, but I protested that Berry had liked my joke. He had thrown back his head and laughed heartily, ending in a falsetto no white man would have used without the risk of appearing "fruity."

As I got older I learned that one does not make such jokes, and so I became more conventionally polite with him. I kept our conversation on surer ground: the weather, the shrubbery, how tired he must get. At midday he would knock on the back door and ask for ice water. I would leave him there and go into the kitchen to take a tray of ice cubes from the freezer, empty them into a bright red plastic pitcher, fill it with cold tap water, and take it out to him, with a glass. As I approached, the rattling of the ice cubes inside the pitcher seemed to make him even thirstier, for his eyes went straight to it and the glass. Then as he ambled off to sit in the shade with his water, I would feel glad to have helped in the household and remember that I would have to be sure that the pitcher and glass were washed extra well that night.

As I got older, Berry came less frequently, because now my parents required me to do some of the yardwork.

It never occurred to me I was horning in on his job — I just hated mowing the lawn. My parents bought him (or perhaps me) a power mower and an electric hedge trimmer. These did not affect his pace in the slightest. He arrived early in the morning and he left late in the afternoon. It was his rhythm.

The only other time we saw him was around Christmas, when he would knock on the back door, hold out his hand palm up, smile his big white-toothed smile, and say, "Christmas present." His ingenuous request invariably struck my mother as funny (without any malice on her part) and after she had given him five or ten dollars and closed the door she would sit down on the couch and, as she put it, "get tickled."

It was rumored that on his own time Berry liked to drink and womanize. He must have had one hell of a winter, because he never worked during the cold months. One winter day, driving through the north side of town, my mother pointed to a one-room shack, isolated on an empty, weedy lot, no car, no phone, and said to me in a hushed tone, "That's where Berry lives." A foreboding, a gloom, an embarrassment came over me. It had never occurred to me to think about where he lived, or under what conditions.

Through all this he never aged and he never showed
even a hint of meanness, envy, or anger, so that for me he
took on an aura of immutability, a sense that in his meas-
ured gait and his seasonal return he was an emissary from
nature itself.

By the time I was twelve, though, I had begun to take
him for granted, like leaves on trees. I paid him less and
less attention. My sense of negritude was awakening in a
more abstract way, at school.

In my grade school there were no blacks, no Catho-
lics, and, so far as I know, no Jews. The schoolwork in-
volving other countries and cultures—China, where the
Chinese live—had the ring of fairy tales. The people different from us were no larger than the illustrations depict-
ing them in our schoolbooks. Likewise, our teachers were
unreal, in that they behaved like teachers, not like people.

Viola Mason was the exception. There were times in
her class when she would put aside the lesson and talk
with us, often about her home life and her two adopted
children. We rejoiced in these sometimes lengthy mono-
logues because they freed us from the stale predictability
of school and made us feel relaxed and personal. Sometimes she would talk about morality and brotherhood.
She awakened in me a sense of the injustice of racial
prejudice.

Naturally I took this home. For instance, when my mother or father used the word "nigger," I got mad and reprimanded them. I lectured them on the Declaration of Independence, the Bill of Rights, the Constitution. They countered my arguments with the most infuriatingly devious adult logic. They knew I was right, but still it was not enough to overcome their relatively moderate prejudice. Our disagreements ended with them feeling relieved that their unsupportable bias was no longer under attack. I came away feeling righteous, chivalrous, and sullen. The sad truth is that aside from Berry I rarely even saw a black person, let alone had one as a friend.

Around the age of fifteen I tried to compensate for this by ostentatiously sitting at the back of the bus, among the blacks, who were as much surprised by this gesture as the white passengers were disgruntled by it. "Among the blacks" is fittingly loose to describe the situation, for, as I wrote in a notebook then, "By nature, if there were only two seats in a bus, one beside a Negro, one beside a white, I would probably choose the white. This I admit." I go on to say, though, that "I have noticed one thing in all my associations with Negroes, on sight I was repelled from them, but after I knew them better, I found them a congenial and reasonable race." Which was awfully white of me. (And I wonder who were all these black people I had gotten to know.) Reading such entries today, I cringe with shame, but I also feel proud of that boy who was struggling to find a way out of his inherited racism, the racism that had become part of his very physiology, his sense of touch, his idea of proximity to a different human body.

Nine months later the same boy wrote an essay called "On Racial Prejudice," which was as much a splenetic attack on "southern ignorance" (including the South's failure to produce large numbers of great writers, musicians, and intellectuals!) as it was a defense of racial equality. After castigating the South for lagging behind the rest of the country "culturally, intellectually, industrially, morally, and politically," I climaxed my diatribe with some fiery but shaky prose:

> But the supreme sin committed by the South is not its refusal to do anything with their minds, to cultivate anything of value in a head filled with prejudice and hard rocks. The worst thing they could have done is to assume a superior position over the Negro population of the South. It's not a sin to be stupid, but when a stupid person tries to illegally dominate and order another sect of the civilization, he has succumbed to the lowest of all scummy tricks. I can't blame the South too much, though, because they have done everything else that is bad and hideous, what

else could they dream up to do in their insidious and brutal minds? The ironic thing is that the Negro seems to be intellectually conquering the white in the South. Many young Negro writers have sprung up in the last two generations. The Negro people are trying to better themselves, and can we blame them for this? Morally, no. But the haughty, domineering southern whites can do anything they wish, even if it is against the wishes of the President they helped elect. They take law into their own stupid hands and say, "To H——— with law and order and justice, we don't want the niggers!" It seems to me that the Negroes should not want the whites, since they have so much more promise for the future. Why can't the stupid people reconcile themselves with the fact that the Negro will in the future intellectually dominate them, that the South is in a recession. Not an economic one, but one far more dangerous to America as a whole: an intellectual slump. But instead of trying to help themselves, they slide ever downwards, and someday will reach the low, low bottom and realize the Negro is better than they are, whether his skin is black or white, he is inside a better person, with more spirit and energy.

In the privacy of my room in our white neighborhood, with no black friends, I was "among the blacks."

I was also among them in being considered a social inferior. Although I was personable and bright, there was an undercurrent in my relationships with my classmates, because my father was stigmatized as a lawbreaker. He earned his living selling whiskey in what was then a "dry" state. No matter how good my grades were, no matter how well I played baseball, no matter how clean my clothes or proper my manners, there was this streak of unspoken social shame that ran through my life outside home and set me apart from others. The parents of some of my friends were wary of me, others would not invite me to their homes or allow me to ride in their cars. Over the next few years, as my rebellious taste for individualism and poetry deepened, as my hair grew longer than acceptable, as I openly rejected materialism, I was to feel even more deeply this gulf between me and white society. To borrow the title of a Norman Mailer essay (which I eagerly read when it was first published), I was becoming a "white negro." So if the blacks were forced to suffer back among the fumes and noise and heat of the bus's internal combustion engine, I would suffer with them. Not one black ever said a word to me on these rides to and from downtown.

One summer day about this time I went on a long bicycle ride around town. I rode through newer middle-class neighborhoods, down toward an older, respectable part of town where my great-aunt and great-uncle lived.

Then I swung north and went for about three miles, to Niggertown. In the late afternoon I rode right down Greenwood Avenue, past rundown businesses, pool rooms, corner groceries, shine parlors, and tiny ramshackle frame houses with people sitting on the porch waiting for a cool breeze, in rocking chairs, on broken-down sofas, on wooden boxes, staring quietly at the street that had little more than cracks and weeds and an occasional passerby. How strange it must have been for them to see a skinny white boy wearing a white tee shirt, white gym trunks, and white sneakers, pedaling along, hardly daring to look to either side. At the intersection ahead I saw women leaning out of the second-story windows of a red brick building. As my bare, bony legs pedaled me by, the women whistled and laughed and called out, "Hey white boy, c'mon back hea'! Hey-ooo, c'mon back, white boy!" I secretly pedaled faster and decided not to think about how shaken I was, or how my feeling for brotherhood had been put to the reality test and found lacking in substance.

By this time rock 'n' roll had hit Tulsa, bringing rhythm 'n' blues along with it. I had "flipped" over Little Richard, Chuck Berry, and Fats Domino, and I had a sneaky fascination for the "dirty" songs ("Work with Me, Annie" and "Annie Had a Baby") by a group called the Midnighters. Also on the radio were old standbys like Sarah Vaughn, Duke Ellington, and Nat "King" Cole. These three were a bit too grownup for me, and Louis Armstrong puzzled me : I liked his voice but I didn't know what to *do* with him. For me there was nothing to compare with the screaming energy of Little Richard or the driving rhythm of Chuck Berry (unless it was the white man's version : Jerry Lee Lewis). A year later, with adolescent imperiousness, I renounced all rock 'n' roll.

It was replaced by black folk music and blues — Lightning Hopkins, Sonny Terry, Brownie McGhee, Muddy Waters, John Lee Hooker, the Reverend Gary Davis, Odetta, Blind Lemon Jefferson, and the immortal Leadbelly, whose every song on the four-record collection called *Leadbelly's Last Sessions* I learned by heart. I also discovered black jazz — Miles Davis, the Modern Jazz Quartet, Chico Hamilton, and Art Blakey's Jazz Messengers. And I discovered the white man's romance with negritude, in the novels of Jack Kerouac, a romance that suited my adolescent soul, a romance of cool, hip, bop, and funk. The black people in Tulsa seemed a mess, but Kerouac confirmed my belief in their spiritual superiority.

Integration came to Tulsa in 1959. I felt its approach when I went into a restaurant and found on the table a new sign stating that the management reserved the right to refuse service to anyone. It meant just one thing. My blood boiled, I leaped up and berated the manager and stormed out.

The blacks were on their way across town. For the first time in Tulsa, black students enrolled in a white school. That is, among the 2,500 whites of Central High School there were now two blacks, a boy, whom I never got to know, and Peaches Littlejohn, who was in my homeroom and French class. It was feared that their presence would cause some kind of racial explosion, but nothing happened. I remember letting my eyes wander up to where Peaches sat, in the first seat of the middle row, in front of Miss Quesenbery's desk, and gazing at her simply because she didn't look like everyone else. She turned out to be nice, polite, a good student: the opposite of inflammatory. I liked her, but it never occurred to me to ask her for a date because my heart was in the throes of love for another girl (who was of course white). Later, heading east to college, I ran into Peaches on the train, on her way to college in St. Louis. This encounter seemed like a good omen, and it made me feel worldly.

My destination was New York, the proverbial melting pot. Except some of the ingredients hadn't melted. Sunday

morning my first week in town, I got off at the wrong
subway stop and walked through a deserted park where a
big black man came up behind me and put a knife to my
throat and demanded money. I had only 65 cents in my
pocket, but I had the nerve to ask him to give me back
a nickel, for coffee. "Here, take a dime," he said. "It's a
dime if you have just coffee at the counter." Then he told
me to walk straight ahead and not to look back or he'd kill
me. His abrupt changes from mugger to counsellor to
murderer seemed unusual, but I decided to think about it
later. It was my first visit to Harlem. It was the first time I
remember being physically touched by a black person.

If New York was not a melting pot, it was a mixing
bowl, with a startling variety of races. I was having the
almost daily experience of seeing people who looked like
people I had known in Tulsa. At Broadway and 114 Street I
was electrified by a woman who bore an absolutely perfect
resemblance to my mother, except that her skin was black.
(A few years later I learned that there was a Ronald Padgett, a black kid the same age as me, living in Harlem.)

At an art opening I met LeRoi Jones, with whom I
had corresponded and whose poetry I had published in a
magazine I edited in high school. Later I met another poet
I had known only by mail, Lorenzo Thomas, and was

jolted to see that he was black—there had been no hint of it in his letters or his poetry. My ignorance had enabled me to correspond with him without racial selfconsciousness, and so when we met we were already on our way to being friends.

Although Columbia College, where I was studying, was all male and mostly white, it was part of a university whose students came from all over the world. In the spring of my sophomore year I shared a room with a (white) classmate whose girlfriend was from Barbados, a tall, beautiful girl with *café au lait* skin. She lived downstairs in the same building, and my roommate spent much of his time with her. At one point I noticed he was acting strange toward me, sullen and furtive. After a few days of this I asked him what was going on. Had I said something that had offended him? Left my socks in his soup? My attempt at humor fell flat. He forced himself to speak. He and his girlfriend had come back to her room and found a handwritten note taped to the door: "Nigger get out." I asked him what that had to do with me. He replied that he was sure that I and a friend had done it, perhaps as a practical joke that had backfired. I tried to assure him that not only had we not done it, that we would *not* have done it—it was not sufficiently witty for us. It was repugnant *and* doltish! He was unconvinced. I gave him my solemn pledge of honor that we were not guilty, but he would have none of it. In his heart he had already made up his mind, and even if his mind were to change, the damage had been done to his feelings toward me. I had to resign myself to losing his trust, but I could not overcome my chagrin that racism had been the cause of it.

The distance between many blacks and whites lengthened in the next few years. Some blacks changed their names and said things such as "All white men are faggots." Although I understood that in politics you use hyperbole and distortion to make a point, to catalyze your constituency, and to gain power, I was resolutely against it. I felt, perhaps naïvely, that in the long run social justice could best be served by a clear, accurate, beautiful use of the language. But I had no quarrel with the rage of the Black Power movement. In fact I was surprised that it hadn't erupted with such intensity long before. In any case, for the next few years blacks and whites were like those little magnetic Scottie dogs that, brought back to back, repel each other. Although in Tulsa I had been called "nigger-lover," now I was a "honky." (Both descriptions were true.) I felt rejected.

So it was that when my son went to kindergarten I was pleased in general by the racial variety of his school and in particular by the fact that his first and best friend there was black, or at least what society still calls black: his mother was Danish and his father Afro-American.

In the meantime I had started teaching poetry writing to children in a school in our neighborhood, mostly children of color. After a few years in the same school I got to know a lot of them, aged six through twelve, and it was then I first felt the joyous relaxation of being blind to color. The children were still young enough not to have sensed the color line so strongly — they accepted me simply as "the poetry man." Like most children, they were freely tactile. The kindergarteners would cling to my legs and feel of my scratchy beard, the second graders would unconsciously play with the buttons on my shirt cuffs when I bent over their desks to help them with a poem, the sixth graders would arm wrestle with me. I noticed that their hands were always warm. I grew very fond of some of these kids. I didn't want them to leave the school and go on to junior high. Invariably my eyes filled with tears at their graduation ceremonies.

In the mid-1970s my wife, son, and I lived for several years in South Carolina, where I was working. It was strange and interesting to come from New York to live in a small textile-mill town in the real South. I expected to see the ignorant, beefy, redneck sheriffs depicted on television and in the movies. I expected to find blacks so down-trodden as to be hopelessly alienated from white society. I expected to come face to face with the South I had excoriated in my teenage essay. I did not expect to find white liberals. I did not expect to find blacks I could be friends with. And particularly I did not expect it to happen on a tennis court.

The public tennis courts were the town's social leveller. It did not matter if you were rich or poor, male or female, black or white. All that mattered was your game. And since it was a relatively small town (population: 10,000) you tended to see the same people at the courts, and to get to know some of them.

This is how I met Zack Jones. Zack was a big, tall, whoppingly powerful young guy, jet black. He wasn't highly educated, but he was intelligent, with perfect instincts, a good heart, and an easy sociability. We spent many hours together. After tennis we would often sit on the court and talk, or he'd come over to my place for a beer or later dinner, and sometimes I'd drive him across town to where he lived, in a small stucco house in a black neighborhood. People there were out late, hanging around, smoking, talking in the warm night. I remember the faces lit up by my car's headlights as I pulled up to drop him off. After the first time, Zack laughed and said, "Dudes can't figure out who this weird white guy is!" When it came to race, Zack was nobody's fool, but his experience hadn't dulled his simple pleasure in liking people, no matter what color. It was as if he had kept alive a part of his innocence, and in this he was like my students in New York. I felt good around him, I was refreshed by his healthy unpretentiousness, and I liked him. He liked me too.

Zack reminded me of George Spenser, a guy who used to play in a poker game that ran every Friday night for around twelve years, a game mostly of writers and artists. Spenser went about six-six, 220, solid muscle on a splendidly proportioned body, topped by a shaved head shining very dark brown. He looked like *the* guy you wouldn't want to meet in a dark alley, but in fact he was a sweet man who loved to play poker and the horses. The rest of us (all white) would come to the game with fifty, maybe sixty dollars. Spencer would walk in with four or five hundred. There was a natural largesse about him, including the way he treated other people. One night he bluffed me out of a hand and cackled as he raked in the chips. I looked at him and said with a smile, "You big black bully!" and he almost rolled off the chair. You don't meet a lot of people like him, darkly sunny.

•

The faces of black people in New York don't look very sunny. They often look pained, hostile, insolent, or aloof, though sometimes when you say something pleasant to them their faces immediately become neutral or even friendly. I suppose that any people treated so poorly for so long would assume a negative public cast, but it's also possible that I project these attributes onto their features, and by expecting unfriendliness I induce or bring it out.

I also expect black men to be big. To me they sometimes look larger than they really are: tall, with bull necks, high derrières, and long legs, with the sleekness of basketball players, the languidness of a Caribbean shoreline beneath a full moon, and the strength of a Mack truck. Unlike white men, they seem to occupy every bit of space inside their skin. It's as if pressure has built up inside their skulls, pushing the features out and forward, stretching the skin taut across the bone, smooth and clear. The hands often hang extra loose at the wrist, palms white, fingernails long, like those of the Masai and Watusi tribal dancers I saw in movies as a child.

Other Africans went elsewhere, and seem to look different for it: witness the range of shimmering copper, mocha, and tan of Martiniquans. In *Two Years in the French West Indies* (1890), Lafcadio Hearn becomes rhapsodic about these luminous shades, so dewy and unlike anything in Europe or North America. I was surprised to find such tones still fresh in Martinique: the girl in a white cotton dress who served me pastry and Nescafé in Morne-Rouge, her eyes blue, then green, then brown against her lightly burnished face reflecting sunlight from the street; the saleswoman in a light pink smock in a stationery shop in Fort de France, her face a dark smouldering brown with magenta underglow; the slender old man in a straw hat in the parking lot in Diamant, his skin a rich, espresso-brown leather and his eyes, yellow with brown irises. It's as though these people could not exist elsewhere in the world, just as the pastel colors of their houses and sunsets seem intrinsic to that locale, unexportable.

In Martinique I was a tourist, which for me is always a little embarrassing. I don't want to stand out from the crowd, selfconsciously aware that I have only the feeblest reasons for being there. But in countries such as Martinique it is impossible for me to blend in: I am white, I have more money than the average Martiniquan, and I am so obviously from another country. I don't even re-semble the other white people there, the French. It is as if I am a jigsaw puzzle piece whose shape fits its space, but whose lines and colors are those of another, different puzzle.

I wish the entire world were made of pieces inter-changeable among all puzzles. I like to be at home among Vermont loggers, Scottish aristocrats, Colombian house-maids, and Chinese photographers. I love it when people very unlike me like me. So because I can't be anyone other than who I am, because I can't switch races or pre-tend I don't come from a particular social class, I yearn for those moments when the other person looks at me and sees a man around forty, tall, slender, with short silver hair and wearing wire-rimmed glasses for eyes that look straight out, and likes the fact that I too am different.

Afterword

RON PADGETT

I first read about Raymond Roussel's "Among the Blacks" in his essay *Comment j'ai écrit certains de mes livres,* in which he describes "a very special method" he used to generate that story:

I chose two almost identical words (reminiscent of metagrams). For example, *billard* (billiard table) and *pillard* (plunderer). To these I added similar words capable of two different meanings, thus obtaining two almost identical phrases.

In the case of *billard* and *pillard* the two phrases I obtained were:

1. *Les lettres du blanc sur les bandes du vieux billard...*

[The white letters on the cushions of the old billiard table...]

2. *Les lettres du blanc sur les bandes du vieux pillard...*

[The white man's letters on the hordes of the old plunderer...]

In the first, "lettres" was taken in the sense of lettering, "blanc" in the sense of a cube of chalk, and "bandes" as in billiard cushions.

In the second, "lettres" was taken in the sense of missives, "blanc" as in white man, and "bandes" as in hordes.

> The two phrases found, it was a case of writing a story which could begin with the first and end with the second.[1]

I thought it would be challenging to translate "Among the Blacks" into English. My first translation managed to get the word play of the story's first and last sentences, but it was marred by errors and uneven diction. A second version, a few years later, corrected some of these problems. Twelve years after that, I looked again and noticed new problems, along with poor solutions to old ones. So I set about coming up with the "final" version, the once-and-for-all perfect translation that matches the formality of the original without sounding stiff. As usual, I am satisfied with the result, but I have no doubt that some day I will read it and grimace and start tinkering with it again. Perhaps at some point I will learn the original language (not to mention my own) well enough to be done with these spells. Or perhaps it is all just an incurable case of "translatoritis."

Unlike the Roussel, my little memoir (which for convenience I'll label "Among the Blacks II") came from the ordinary urge to express a cluster of personal feelings and ideas. Specifically, it grew out of the nagging need to come to grips with the frustration of being a white American who had grown up in a racist environment and who, despite his rejection of racism at an early age, had rarely felt unselfconscious in the company of a black person. As such, "Among the Blacks II" is an unstylized outpouring of feeling, an attempt simply to tell the truth, and to do so with a minimum of artfulness. In writing it, I found myself trying to keep the prose as transparent and un-mannered as possible, not because I had a preconceived notion of how to proceed, but because that's the way it happened. Theoretically, a "clean" style suits an "honest" confession. Whether or not the piece succeeds is, of course, another matter.

There is also the question of what perversity drove me to give it the same title as Roussel's story, and then to compound the confusion by giving the same name to the volume that contains them both. It was probably less the intellectual devilishness that inspired Borges to create a Pierre Menard who would write *Don Quixote*, word for word, and call it a new book, than it was an orneriness that allowed me to take a fiendish pleasure at the thought of librarians and bibliographers gnashing their teeth and cursing the name of Padgett for his having done this to them. Being forced to refer to my piece as "Among the Blacks II" in this note, though, I see I've already been hoisted by my own petard.

Other than superficiality of subject matter—white man among blacks—the two pieces have little in common, unless it be their diametrical opposition. Roussel's is a calculated, formal, distanced, armored, and secretly insane work of fiction; mine is a spontaneous, casual, personal, vulnerable, and openly neurotic memoir. Like magnetic Scottie dogs turned to face each other, perhaps these opposites attract. I hope that the proximity of two such different pieces will serve to clarify both, or at least allow them to act as mutual foils.

Ultimately, I just like to see what happens when two disparate things are put together. When I was little, one of my favorite books had pages that, cut horizontally into three parts, enabled the reader to mix and mismatch the heads, torsos, and legs of various characters, and I never tire of the Surrealist game of *cadavres exquis* (exquisite corpses), in which a similar procedure is applied to syntax. In thinking about these juxtapositions, I'm reminded of what Reverdy said about the poetic image :

> It cannot be born from a comparison, but rather from the bringing together of two realities that are more or less distant from each other.
>
> The more distant and correct the relationships between these realities, the more emotive power and poetic reality the image will have.

He goes on to say, though, that

> Two realities that have no relationship cannot be brought together usefully. No image is created.
> Two contrary realities cannot be brought together. They oppose each other.[2]

In this volume, I wanted to bring together two opposite— but not contrary—realities, to place them side by side and see how, in forming a third entity, they change each other. I leave it to others to decide whether that has happened here, and whether it was worth the effort.

—*R.P.*

---

1. Roussel's essay was published posthumously in 1935. This translation, by Trevor Winkfield, is from *How I Wrote Certain of My Books* (New York: SUN, 1975), p. 3.

2. "L'Image" in *Nord-Sud, self defence, et autres écrits sur l'art et la poésie (1917–1926)* (Paris: Flammarion, 1975), p. 73. My translation.